Hello, Family Members,

Learning to read is one of the most important accomplishments of early childhood. **Hello Reader!** books are designed to help children become skilled readers who like to read. Beginning readers learn to read by remembering frequently used words like "the," "is," and "and"; by using phonics skills to decode new words; and by interpreting picture and text clues. These books provide both the stories children enjoy and the structure they need to read fluently and independently. Here are suggestions for helping your child *before*, *during*, and *after* reading:

Before
- Look at the cover and pictures and have your child predict what the story is about.
- Read the story to your child.
- Encourage your child to chime in with familiar words and phrases.
- Echo read with your child by reading a line first and having your child read it after you do.

During
- Have your child think about a word he or she does not recognize right away. Provide hints such as "Let's see if we know the sounds" and "Have we read other words like this one?"
- Encourage your child to use phonics skills to sound out new words.
- Provide the word for your child when more assistance is needed so that he or she does not struggle and the experience of reading with you is a positive one.
- Encourage your child to have fun by reading with a lot of expression...like an actor!

After
- Have your child keep lists of interesting and favorite words.
- Encourage your child to read the books over and over again. Have him or her read to brothers, sisters, grandparents, and even teddy bears. Repeated readings develop confidence in young readers.
- Talk about the stories. Ask and answer questions. Share ideas about the funniest and most interesting characters and events in the stories.

I do hope that you and your child enjoy this book.

—Francie Alexander
Chief Education Officer,
Scholastic's Learning Ventures

For Martha Bartenbach, librarian, and for all the kids at the United Nations School, Queens, New York
—K.M.

For the Doughertys
—M.S.

Author's note:
The story "Fluffy Meets a Leprechaun" is loosely based on T. Crofton Croker's "The Field of Boliauns," in *Legends and Traditions of the South of Ireland* (1825).

No part of this publication may be reproduced, or stored in a retrieval system, or transmitted in any form or by any means, electronic, mechanical, photocopying, recording, or otherwise, without written permission of the publisher. For information regarding permission, write to Scholastic Inc., Attention: Permissions Department, 555 Broadway, New York, NY 10012.

ISBN 0-439-31944-7

Text copyright © 2002 by Kate McMullan.
Illustrations copyright © 2002 by Mavis Smith.
All rights reserved. Published by Scholastic Inc.
SCHOLASTIC, HELLO READER, CARTWHEEL BOOKS, and associated logos are trademarks and/or registered trademarks of Scholastic Inc.

Library of Congress Cataloging-in-Publication Data

McMullan, Kate.
    Fluffy's lucky day / by Kate McMullan; illustrated by Mavis Smith.
      p. cm. — (Hello reader! Level 3)
    Summary: On the day of the school's Saint Patrick's Day party, Fluffy the classroom guinea pig learns about and meets a leprechaun.
    ISBN 0-439-31944-7
      [1. Guinea pigs—Fiction. 2. Leprechauns—Fiction. 3. Saint Patrick's Day—Fiction. 4. Schools—Fiction] I. Smith, Mavis, ill. II. Title. III. Hello reader! Level 3.
PZ7.M2295 Ffh 2002
[E]—dc21   2001049033

10 9 8 7 6 5 4 3 2   02 03 04 05 06

Printed in the U.S.A.   24
First printing, March 2002

FLUFFY'S
LUCKY DAY

by Kate McMullan
Illustrated by Mavis Smith

Hello Reader! — Level 3

SCHOLASTIC INC.
New York   Toronto   London   Auckland   Sydney
Mexico City   New Delhi   Hong Kong   Buenos Aires

I Love Green!

"Today is our lucky day,"
Ms. Day told her class.
It is? thought Fluffy. **Oh, boy!**

"We have a visitor from Ireland," said Ms. Day. "This is Mr. Kelly, Jasmine's grandfather. He has come to tell us about St. Patrick's Day and about the green land of Ireland."
I love green, thought Fluffy.

Mr. Kelly had on a green shirt
and a green vest. He had on green
pants and green shoes.
He wore a red scarf
around his neck.
"Top of the morning to you,"
said Mr. Kelly. "I love green."
Me, too! thought Fluffy.

"Ireland has green, green grass," said Mr. Kelly.

I love grass! thought Fluffy.

"Ireland has hills of green clover," said Mr. Kelly.

I love clover! thought Fluffy. **Take me to Ireland!**

"On St. Patrick's Day,"
said Mr. Kelly,
"everyone in Ireland wears green—
even the leprechauns."

He walked to Fluffy's play yard. He picked Fluffy up. He said, "A leprechaun is a 'wee one' no bigger than this guinea pig."
Hey, who are you calling a wee one? thought Fluffy.

"Leprechauns always tell the truth,"
said Mr. Kelly. "They are grumpy.
And very rich. Every leprechaun
has a pot of gold."
"I wish I had a pot of gold,"
said Emma.
"Me, too!" everyone said. "Me, too!"
Fluffy was not sure what gold was.
But everyone wanted a pot of it.
So Fluffy wanted one, too.

"If you catch a leprechaun, you can get his gold," said Mr. Kelly.
"How?" asked Maxwell.
Yeah, how? thought Fluffy.

"Keep your eye on him,"
said Mr. Kelly.
"He cannot disappear
while you are looking at him.
He will try to get away. Oh, yes!
He will try to trick you. But keep
looking at him. At last he will
give up and show you
where his gold is hidden."

"Have you ever seen
a leprechaun?" asked Wade.
"I've caught one!" said Mr. Kelly.
"He is in my pocket."
Mr. Kelly reached into his pocket.
"Come out, Tom!" he said.
Fluffy's eyes grew big.
He couldn't wait to see a wee one!

"Oh, my stars," said Mr. Kelly.
"Tom has disappeared!
If you see him, keep your eye
on him and catch him!"

Fluffy did not see Tom.
But he hoped he would.
Then he would catch him
and get his pot of gold.
After all, thought Fluffy,
today is my lucky day!

Fluffy Meets a Leprechaun

"Will you stay for our
St. Patrick's Day party?"
Ms. Day asked Mr. Kelly.
"We're having green cupcakes,"
said Emma.
"With green sprinkles," said Jasmine.
"I'll stay!" said Mr. Kelly.

Fluffy closed his eyes.
He pictured Ireland. He saw
green grass. And green clover.
And green beans. And all sorts
of good green things to eat.
Fluffy saw himself dressed in green
with a red scarf around his neck.

Fluffy walked down a green road.
He heard a noise: *tap, tap, tap*.
Fluffy looked behind a bush.
A leprechaun! thought Fluffy.

Top of the morning to you, leprechaun! Fluffy said.

The leprechaun jumped.

Oh, my stars! he said.

Fluffy looked at the leprechaun.

Where is your pot of gold? Fluffy said.

Over there, said the leprechaun.
He pointed. **In the field. See it?**
Fluffy was about to turn his head.
Then he remembered. He had
to keep looking at the leprechaun!

You can't trick me, said Fluffy.
He kept his eyes on the leprechaun.
I give up, said the leprechaun.
I will take you to my gold.
Fluffy smiled. **Let's go!** he said.

The leprechaun led Fluffy
to a field of weeds.
My gold is buried here, he said.
Under this weed.
Fluffy knew the leprechaun
was telling the truth.
I will get a shovel, Fluffy said.
I will dig up your gold!

Fluffy had to find this weed again.
So he tied his red scarf to it.
**Do not take the scarf off
while I am gone,** said Fluffy.
I won't, said the leprechaun.

Fluffy knew the leprechaun
was telling the truth.
He ran home for a shovel.
But when he came back,
he got a big surprise.

A red scarf just like his
was tied to every weed!
Which weed was it? said Fluffy.
There was no way to tell.

The leprechaun told the truth,
thought Fluffy.
But he tricked me!
Now I will never
find his pot of gold!
Fluffy heard someone laughing.
He knew it was the leprechaun!

Fluffy's Lucky Day

The laughing grew louder.
Fluffy opened his eyes.
He was not in green, green Ireland.
He was in his play yard.

All the kids were laughing.
They were having their
St. Patrick's Day party.
I guess I am not invited,
thought Fluffy.
This is NOT my lucky day!

Fluffy went to his food bowl.
He looked in it. He saw something!
A leprechaun! said Fluffy.

Go away, said the leprechaun.
I am taking a nap.
Fluffy said, **Are you Tom?**
The leprechaun said,
Maybe yes, maybe no.
Why should I tell you?

You ARE Tom, said Fluffy.
And you are grumpy.
Tom frowned. **So what?** he said.
All leprechauns are grumpy.

All leprechauns are rich, too, said Fluffy. **I want your gold!** Tom pointed to the far end of the play yard. **A pot of gold is over there,** he said. **But it is YOUR gold.** Fluffy smiled. **You can't trick me,** he said. **I will not look over there.**

Have it your way,
said the leprechaun.
**But I'm telling you
the pot of gold is there.
And leprechauns always
tell the truth.**

Is this a trick? Fluffy wondered.
He tried to keep one eye on Tom.
He tried to look at the pot of gold
with the other eye.
But he could not do it.

I am going to look, said Fluffy.
Do you promise not to move while I turn my head to look?
Tom nodded. **I promise,** he said.
Fluffy knew the leprechaun was telling the truth.

Fluffy turned his head.
He saw a little pot!
Could it be a pot of gold?
Fluffy turned back to Tom.

But Tom was gone.

Hey! said Fluffy. **You promised!**

Fluffy heard Tom laughing.

I promised not to move while you turned your head to look, said Tom. **But I never said I wouldn't move while you turned your head back!**

Rats! thought Fluffy.
Tricked again!
He ran over to the pot.
He looked inside.

Inside the pot
were bits of golden corn.
So this is gold! thought Fluffy.
"Happy St. Patrick's Day, Fluffy!"
said all the kids.

What do you know?
thought Fluffy
as he ate some corn.
It's my lucky day after all.